Other Books in the Series:

THE SOUTH OF
BLACK
FORGIVENESS

Dr. Donna Clovis

BALBOA.PRESS

A DIVISION OF HAY HOUSE

This is a work of fiction. All of the characters, names, incidents, organizations, and dialogue in this novel are either the products of the author's imagination or are used fictitiously.

Balboa Press books may be ordered through booksellers or by contacting:

Balboa Press
A Division of Hay House
1663 Liberty Drive
Bloomington, IN 47403
www.balboapress.com
1 (877) 407-4847

Print information available on the last page.

ISBN: 978-1-9822-4347-0 (sc)
ISBN: 978-1-9822-4349-4 (hc)
ISBN: 978-1-9822-4348-7 (e)

Library of Congress Control Number: 2020903397

Balboa Press rev. date: 02/20/2020

In a bustling New York scene, a young African American journalist who survives her darkest moment alone, becomes the target of a heinous crime.

Dedicated to my husband James,

children Michaela, Justin, and Matthian,

my parents and in-laws who are the past, present, and future

of my lifetime

And my editor, Gabriella Oldham

INTRODUCTION

His black female victims are invisible in the darkness until the police officer sees them. But film itself erases their existence by not bothering to show them as human as they truly are. When White supremacy goes unchecked, it becomes this delusional space that illuminates and occupies part of a society like film. For whiteness is the hidden accomplice that fosters the violence one sees onscreen.

CONTENTS

CHAPTER 1

CAGES AND CUFFS

It seemed like an army ambush: seven cops, two squad cars, and two supervising officers rushed to cuff a young Black teen at the #1 subway station at 110th Cathedral Parkway for fare evasion of $2.75.

As a few community members watched and videotaped the arrest, they followed the police presence and procession into the precinct. Suddenly, a wrinkled black scrawny hand crept carefully upon the police desk unveiling a one-hundred-dollar bill, saying, "Sirs, please pay his subway fare and give him the rest to make it back home."

And another community elder yelled, "Hey, fare evasion in this city is a hundred bucks for the ticket with no jail time."

"Let him go." A few people persisted showing the video on their phones.

And he was released without further incident. For this is a deeply entrenched problem. Racism is woven into the police culture and it is easily proven to be lethal most times.

CHAPTER 2

SILENT KILLER

B ut the silent killer in the darkness of the community is a sociopath. One who blends in with the beggars and prostitutes on the streets. One who actually befriends them using whiteness in a treachery grinning. But the streets pretend not to know the murderous acts behind the slicing screams of blackness in the dark. A murder is suddenly illuminated by the flashlight of a cop discovering a prostitute's black lifeless body in the grunge of a nearby alleyway.

CHAPTER 3

LIGHTNING

The next morning, the trees in the park lift their wet red blood tresses of leaves blown up by the wind and shudder in the flash of lightning illuminating black faces walking. The lightning leaves the air with an aroma of ozone in autumn.

And within this darkened realm of Morningside Heights near 125th Street in Harlem, they are killing blackness. The unarmed murdered people here are all Black.

CHAPTER 4

THE COLOR OF FEAR

And the outside door was ajar and the light leaked from the inside out. And it was the light that always peers into the darkness as it exposes the black body to the cop's sight and the assumption that the intruders are the people living in the residence.

But it was a well-meaning welfare call of innocence of a concerned neighbor that cried a non-emergency number for help.

And soon in the darkness, he sees a shadow. There is no shouting before attempting to walk into a child's dark bedroom. But the blackness is threatening enough as he blackens out and the flashlight obscures her face through the window, shouting, "Put your hands up! Let me see your hands!" Four seconds—shots fired through a back window. And a thud of a sudden collapse.

When the color of your skin is seen as a weapon, one has already lost the fight for a self-defense.

CHAPTER 5

SUNNY DAYS

The design of Sesame Street was based on the brownstones found in Harlem. Getting to Harlem was much like taking Duke Ellington's A train uptown in the subway. This is how Tanisha started her work life in New York as a journalist. She had just finished her schooling at the J-School at Columbia University and embarked on an internship on the *Sesame Street* set in Queens where she met characters like the Grouch and Bert who were orange and green and could cross all racial color lines.

Now as a full-fledged journalist, Tanisha started as a reporter for a small local newspaper called *The Columbia Herald* and settled in a brownstone on the border of Harlem that she always admired the Muppets for inhabiting.

CHAPTER 6

A PRESS CONFERENCE

T he bare police auditorium was noisy with the rapid-fire clicks of the camera shutters taking photos with the bustling conversation of the press crowd that had gathered with their camera men. Soon the noise was quieted to chatter and then a hush by the booming voice of the police chief into the blaring microphone.

"Thank you for joining us this evening. The mayor will give initial statements and then we will open it up to questions," the Chief of Police started and then left the podium for the mayor to stand.

"On behalf of this entire city, I am sorry. What happened Saturday night was undeserving. I am apologizing to the entire city, my city." The mayor shook his head from side to side and then sat down with the audience as the Chief of Police returned to the podium.

"The officer who shot the innocent victim in her own home resigned last night. He has been handcuffed, arrested, and charged with murder. He has been a cop for 18 months with the department. I would like to open the floor to questions from the press," he said as he viewed the sudden rush in the room for frantically waving their hands in the air.

"Let's start here, in the corner," the Chief of Police pointed.

An old Black man with a backwards baseball cap stood up. "Haven't there been a number of killings by cops lately?' he asked in a gruff voice.

"Yes, we are investigating," the police chief said.

"When do you think it is appropriate to shoot into a dark bedroom of a child?" another woman stood up and shouted.

"It isn't," he said. "We must check the surroundings first."

"And was there a gun found?" another voice yelled out.

"On the floor of the bedroom."

"Doesn't the family want an independent investigation?" a tall White man in a three-piece suit asked deliberately.

"We are investigating."

"How dangerous is it for Black people to live in this city anymore? Last month, even the witness to the last major murder was killed and we suspect the cops who have no explanation for it have something to do with that." Another Black old man nodded and looked around the room as it murmured.

"But why didn't the police simply knock at the door first?" a Black woman with a blonde weave stood up and said looking at her notepad.

There was a sudden hush in the room as the woman peered over her blue-framed glasses, "Isn't that obvious?"

"We are looking at the evidence."

"And wasn't the officer already released on bail anyway? We have the FOIA documents. And what about this crumbled note left at the crime scene. It asked for forgiveness. It said I am sorry. Forgive me.

It was typed in a varied font. Anyone address this?" Her questions went out rapid fire into the air of the stifling room.

There was an awkward silence.

"The FBI found the note. We are investigating," the Chief of Police said.

"But he fired his service weapon before identifying himself as an officer. Someone answer me. It's right here in the report. Isn't this a serious problem?" Tanisha asked, taking off her glasses.

"We are investigating," the Chief of Police repeated.

"And that's all they have to say," yelled a tall White man in a gray suit from across the room said as he slammed his fist against the table. "Isn't that always the way? Everyone needs to note that the cop resigned because he was about to be fired. He should have been fired. No justice. No peace!"

"But answer me, why was the cop parked around the corner, creeping around? Do cops have the authority to enter a backyard and then shoot through a dark window? And the cop is allowed to obliterate the woman's face with the light from a flashlight at close range? That's the last she saw in the dark before she was shot," Tanisha argued with a huge sigh.

"We have called in the FBI," the Chief of Police said.

And the room grew silent.

CHAPTER 7

MEETING

They had never met before today, never spoken, but their lives were already intertwined somehow into a disquieting one.

"You seem to know a lot about this case," the older White man said to Tanisha.

"Just as much as anyone else," she glared back as she packed her briefcase and closed it.

"A little testy today? I am here for the same reasons. I'm Jonathan and very nice to meet you. I'm a freelancer for the *Post*."

She looked at him from the corner of her eye and smirked. Then she pulled her blonde curls away from her blue glasses. "I'm Tanisha and why am I meeting you?"

"Crime stories. I thought it might be good to make alliances with people. You never know when we need each other. Can we exchange business cards? Everyone does here."

And at that moment the room squeezed in tight and the crowd of journalists enveloped them in a fury of conversation, everyone exchanging cards and cell numbers until Tanisha merged into the blackness of the night.

CHAPTER 8

NEW YORK BUSINESS

It was her everyday color of choice. All black New York business attire. Tanisha could not move outside of fashion's dark color schemes of black, navy, and gray for fall without the bright red lipstick and blonde curly weave that changed her aura into a look of flirtatious and defiant.

She needed the defiance to give her the power-edge style that made her complete with the unusual hue of blue glasses. Her strong persona and this pop of color gave her a twinge that made journalism all business and kept unwanted admirers away.

CHAPTER 9

ZUCKERBERG

"Facebook's Mark Zuckerberg's free expression speech today creates an atmosphere of an assassination. There needs to be an assurance that Black users are not targeted with misinformation, harassment, and censorship on his social media platform and make an effort to stop the alliance with anti-Black forces. Until then, he is an enabler of White supremacy," Tanisha read out loud to her editor. "No tell me I am being too harsh in this Op-Ed piece. I know I am not. There are those that believe black bodies need to be monitored, that they need to be policed. I think Zuckerberg is one of them. Someone has to make a stand."

"I agree, Tanisha. But we must be careful," her editor Tom cautioned. "I think this is good now and we've revised this enough. Let's send this off to copy editing now. Why don't you go home? You've been overworking the last few weeks."

CHAPTER 10

STOIC BROWNSTONES

Tanisha lived on the third floor of one of the few stoic brownstones left over from the Twenties, a stone-age away from the contemporary times of New York City tucked away between office buildings of Columbia University on 120th Street and bordered on the unenchanted middle class.

It was a quiet place where she could live and work while attending grad school at Columbia's J-School. She climbed the front stairs, slowly dragging the tiredness of her body. She had spent several weeks working overtime and was exhausted.

As she reached the top stoop, she greeted the flower with a glance and by now, it had withered with overgrown thorns of protected solitude and silence.

CHAPTER 11

BUSINESS CARDS

He looked out of place. It was cold and pouring rain in the dawn hours of the morning and there was no ledge or porch to protect his head from the water. And when the doorbell rang, Tanisha lingered looking out the peephole, wondering who might venture out on such a dismal day.

When she opened the door, there stood Jonathan leaning against the door in the wetness of his gray three-piece suit with red tie. He sought out her glance in a bashful way. "May I come in? It's wet out here. I wanted to talk some more about the shooting," he said.

"Which shooting? I can't count anymore," Tanisha said sarcastically. "How do you know where I live anyway?"

"Your business card?"

"And maybe I don't want you here right now?"

He shrugged his shoulders for he wasn't ready for that news.

"Why don't we meet in the precinct board room. Call first, maybe we can talk. Are you freelancing a story?" Tanisha asked.

"I am." He smiled.

"Maybe," Tanisha glanced as she shut the front door in his face.

He frowned. Then he pushed himself straight to stand up on both feet. Then walked down the front stairs in the pouring rain.

CHAPTER 12

THE HUG

There exists the feel of a warm burly hug of an embrace. It was one of great relief as the sigh of a forgiveness exhaled. She felt the air squeezed from her limp white body into warm brown flesh. "And that is how it begins as an endearment from an African American female judge to a White female officer just convicted of the crime of murder of an innocent Black man eating ice cream on the sofa of his own home," the news commentator said.

And the voices on the television continued talking as a continued overwhelming rumbling as Tanisha tried to remove the clutter of her pots and pans from the sink with clangs and bangs. Then with the water running even louder, she walked from the kitchen into the living room and turned off the television. Now sitting before it, like a magnetized Buddha worshipping, she stared at her own Blackness on the blank screen as the steady hum of static disappeared. And her disbelief of the events became the discontentment that filled her mind as another replay of the original crime.

CHAPTER 13

SUBSCRIPTIONS

Today, President Trump cancels all federal news subscriptions from the *Washington Post* and *New York Times* in an effort to attack media outlets. The White House Press secretary said this is an effort to save taxpayer dollars from the spread of fake news.

CHAPTER 14

BE CAREFUL HOW YOU HANG YOUR DECORATIONS

It is the week before Halloween and there are depictions of brown children hanging from nooses in the New York City school window. Here pumpkins painted with black faces and white eyes are smiling and looking on. Hanging anything from a noose denotes a legacy that haunts us today in a historical imagery. Some have made this holiday scary about very real things and in response, the community is in an outrage. Last night, the decorations were finally taken down.

CHAPTER 15

UNMARKED CARS

Cops in unmarked cars grab a group of Black children out for trick or treating in an affluent neighborhood of Brooklyn. The police line them up against a wall to search and handcuff them. They bring them into the local precinct, crying, and finally release them without charges.

CHAPTER 16

BRUTALITY

It is an atrocity when parents of Black and Latino children are relieved after an encounter with the police—that their children are alive, not shot dead.

This brutality must stop.

CHAPTER 17

BOWELS OF INNER EARTH

In this city, blackness coexists within the bowels of inner urban Earth's dirt basements and cement encastled behind lofty walls of tenement scaffolding white windows.

Life lies and crawls as roaches encroached beneath its cramped spaces of motives and movements in the shadows of an unequal world surviving.

And in the sweetness of a light perfume, the meticulous hands fidget with a nervous obsessive compulsion for bomb-making materials as timers, nails, and explosives. As one shudders the panning of the window like a camera motion twitching like the watching of a Hitchcock flick pretending, a sanctified pose in prayer.

CHAPTER 18

HEADLINE

The entire N-word was spelled out in a headline. The copy editor was incensed, but the head editor had excused it. The article had been printed in its entirety.

All of the editors in the newsroom of the *Patriot Ledger* in Massachusetts were White and what one journalist hated was the tolerance of racist news stories. And this copy editor quit his job to protest what African Americans face every day telling the news.

Diversity is more than having Black reporters talk about the news, but to foster an environment and a culture that care for all people and the communities they represent.

And to note, the man who quit his job today is White and Jewish. And he is in need of a job.

CHAPTER 19

TO STUDY

It was 11:30 p.m. An African American college senior passes through the black gates of Columbia University on his way to the library to study for an exam. He carries his ID in his pocket as he always does, but forgets to show it to the security guard as he rushes pass him. Then a faint call of "Sir." But the student is in a hurry and does not hear him.

Then suddenly, the student is pushed to the ground with his head hitting the ground. He lets out a squeal in pain. There are now six security guards on his back. He is pinned to the ground.

Within 24 hours, a video emerges viral showing the scene on campus in the darkness of night. The discussion now on campus—how students of color are treated at its prominent university.

By the end of the week, five security guards and their supervisor are placed on administrative leave. Three undergraduate deans from Columbia University decry racism, calling the incident "disturbing." And full-page stories from *The New York Times* and *Washington Post* are published with headlines.

CHAPTER 20

RIGHTS WITHOUT RESPONSIBILITIES

Journalists have traditionally maintained responsibility for the First Amendment in the United States. The First Amendment is used for democracy and the plurality of opinion in a national conversation. But nowadays, many people are willing to let newspapers die. And Facebook avoids being a truthful media outlet. Its existence is the result of profit making at any cost and a collective refusal of granting fairness in information. It serves as a propaganda machine for politicians running their political ads. On Facebook, real news is propaganda.

CHAPTER 21

QUESTIONS

"Under your policy at Facebook, I can spread political misinformation regarding the 2020 elections. I wanted to see how far I can push this. Can I target Black voters in the wrong zip code and give them incorrect election data?"

"No comment," Mark Zuckerberg said.

"So would you say White supremacists tied to publications met rigorous fact-checking standards?"

"I cannot say."

"So you won't take down the lies. A simple yes or no answer will do."

Silence.

~ C-Span House Financial Committee Meeting and
Mark Zuckerberg,
October 23, 2019.

CHAPTER 22

THE LANGUAGE OF LYNCHING AND SUPREMACY

The last gasps of air from Black bodies hanging describes the picture of a lynching with the formal definition as a systemic form of social control and racial terror. And the term lynching is invoked by powerful people who steal the language of others to make themselves victims. President Trump knows the power of this language. He has used it to compare his plight of impeachment as a lynching. He has used paid ads from the *New York Times* to call for the execution of Black men who were later exonerated.

This carefully crafted narrative perpetuates lynching as beatings, shootings, and torture of Black people in contemporary times. This imaginary victimization inspires vigilantes and White supremacists by any means necessary. It is a dangerous trajectory of a nation.

CHAPTER 23

PLAYGROUND

A White woman confronted a few Black teens at the Morningside Park playground near 118th Street demanding that they leave the children's park. The teens protested by saying they were only playing and not doing anything wrong.

But the angry woman grew more obstinate yelling at the young people, declaring that she was a cop. She ordered them to leave as she grabbed the large swing away from them.

The incident was captured on video and later posted on Twitter. The woman was later arrested and brought into custody for impersonating an officer. And an older warrant caused her to be charged with two DWIs.

CHAPTER 24

ANOTHER OPED

"We need another OpEd," Tanisha complained. "You know that Trump's comparison of a lynching to his own impeachment is just a fast way of creating a news cycle of controversy. Journalists must take a stand."

"I told you, it's already being handled in other papers and it will be repetitive," her editor Tom said, putting his hands on his hips.

"We need more people on this. The hate just escalates. You don't understand," Tanisha said, waving her arms in the air.

"I want you to cover the Elijah Cummings story for Thursday and Friday. Your train leaves for Washington, D.C. by noon today and then to Baltimore. You stay there overnight and everything is set up for you. Get a good story angle. This is big."

CHAPTER 25

THE LEGACY AND LIFE OF AN ELIJAH

There were not enough boxes of tissues to wipe away the floodgates of tears. For Elijah Cummings lies in state on Capitol Hill in Statuary Hall as the first African American in Washington where he spent 23 years serving in Congress. Mourners congregated before dawn as an endless line as it snaked around and throughout the building.

The following day brought the crowds to Baltimore at the New Psalmist Baptist Church. Obama gave the eulogy quoting that Elijah would die for his people as he lived every minute for them. Elijah knew that racism in this country kills and demonstrated the willingness to speak up in a courageous manner for Black survival and triumph.

Today without him, there is a void, but a persistence of his heart in the spirit of justice that is a gift to us who continue to uphold his work. In the silence of a darkness, as Elijah's sheep, we will always hear his voice.

CHAPTER 26

RIDE OF TERROR

It was just a normal subway ride. But it took all of two minutes and twenty seconds to turn the ride into one of terror. People fleeing. Guns drawn. Several Transit police engage in a SWAT-like mission that intends to provoke and escalate a situation as they attempt to arrest a young Black man sitting down in the subway car. Now with his hands in the air, they grab him and pin him to the ground. This is a militarization of the police.

Five hundred more Transit officers have been hired to patrol the New York City subway system. And during the last ten days, the NYPD has shot and killed six more people of color. But the police have just confirmed that this man in this incident has been arrested for fare beating.

CHAPTER 27

CANDLELIGHT VIGIL

A vigil was held for a Black woman who was gunned down last week by a White officer who shot through the back window while the front door was ajar in her own home.

Sage burned and piles of fresh flowers were left at the corner of Amsterdam at 126th Street in Harlem. A procession of about eighty people gathered with yellow candles aglow with wicks whispering a sadness of melancholy.

The event followed with a prayer and a speech by the local pastor. "We never know who will be next. White supremacy has no value for Black lives. The culture of policing has left the community feeling hopeless and living in a war zone."

As the last two mourners walked away for the night, a cinder from their candle blew away, falling alone and melted black cold upon the white concrete sidewalk.

CHAPTER 28

THE AMBER APPEAL AFTER THE MURDER OF A WITNESS

The crime scenes sound like a work of fiction, but the characters and evidence are very real.

Lawyers recently filed an intent to appeal a murder conviction and a ten-year sentence for former officer and murderer, Amber Guyger. Guyger was convicted last month and sentenced for ten years for shooting her Black neighbor when she entered his apartment while he was eating ice cream on the sofa of his own home.

And the key Black male witness to the White cop shooting was then murdered days later as officials do not know who was responsible for the crime. The victim was ambushed and shot in the mouth at close range while leaving his car.

So the saga of a cycle of White violence and Black forgiveness continues without remorse or consequence in a series of uninterrupted instant replays.

CHAPTER 31

THE LOOK OF DRUNKEN BLACKFACE

Tanisha was horrified. She had never seen anything like this. The dark courtyard near the J-School of Columbia was filled with people drunken on blackface, laughing hysterically as if lost in a deranged funhouse of insensibility and hate. She had read about the secret parties at the Princeton campus and their long Southern traditions, but that was the South. That was then as she suddenly realized how much it was part of the tradition infiltrated into the North.

She had walked down this alley past the black gates by accident this night. With her hands over her mouth, she gasped for fear of being heard and throwing up at the same time as she ran slipping through the heat of the darkness.

CHAPTER 32

THE SWORN SECRECIES OF BLACKFACE

The next day, Tanisha committed herself to research at the Columbia library and found the link to the Princeton archives on slavery at Princeton University. The slavery documents provided evidence of the minstrel traditions of blackface so familiar in the South. It was a nostalgic vision to perpetuate slavery and White supremacy through this medium. And they mockingly portrayed free Blacks in northern cities with the same disregard. The town of Princeton was no different. Princeton students touted drunken bouts of blackface and white wigs at frat houses like the Triangle Club on Prospect.

The revelry had spread from the Southern universities to the Ivy leagues including Columbia and Harvard, creating a secret society of racism. And Tanisha trembled at that fact as she cried hysterically. For she had experienced the horror of blackface firsthand.

CHAPTER 33

TWO WEEKS OFF

In the strong white light of her living room, Tanisha looked drawn and tired. It had been two weeks since the blackface incident and she was still reeling from its effects. She had reported it to the police and told her editor Tom, who was willing to give her two weeks paid away and support her with an extra police presence while covering her stories.

But Tanisha worried more about the White people who were in authority and believed in White supremacy who hid behind the blackface that night. But by day, they were more dangerous. They were probably people she knew and she had a gut-wrenching feeling they were people she knew all too well.

CHAPTER 34

FREE SWIPE

J ust saw a policeman give someone a free swipe in the #1 subway station at 116th Street.

CHAPTER 35

RAID

When White cops armed with drawn guns raid a home in Harlem, instead of finding the king-pen of drug lords they are looking for, they find two Black toddlers crying as the cops yell the words, "Get down on the ground!"

The mother in the back bedroom is immediately shoved to the ground and handcuffed when the cops realize they are in the wrong apartment.

A series of wrongful raids of failing to verify address by an informant is traumatizing young children. And police are not keeping track about how often they are getting the raids wrong.

The department is under a new federal consent agreement to make reform to the Peter Mendez Act, a bill to protect children from unreasonable police force and harassment.

CHAPTER 36

EXPLOSION

It was a bright Sunday morning in December and the blinds of Tanisha's apartment filtered silver gray at half-mast. She had stopped attending church three years ago, feeling the need to sleep in every weekend to catch up on her sleep due to a hectic schedule.

But she was awakened this morning by a boom-like explosion of an earthquake that caused her to leap suddenly out of bed. She grabbed her cell phone and thought she would run, but instead looked on Twitter. There was nothing she could find, but as she walked closer to her window, Tanisha could see flames rising and swaying to an unusual height a few blocks away toward Harlem. And then she gasped.

It happened again. A bomb. A shooting. And screaming. Then a White male in guerilla gear shooting again in the open church doors. The gunman fleeing as two White cops in pursuit merged into the cramped streets filled with Sunday vendors of a flea market with clothing racks flying between the cheap five and dime stores.

CHAPTER 37

AFTERMATH

In the aftermath, a total of six parishioners killed and five wounded in the Pentecostal Church storefront. It would have been worse, but a brave soldier visiting from Iraq placed his body in the way to shield the bullets.

And the White gunman cannot be found. The two white cops had shot empty into the Black crowded streets. At the 25th precinct, everyone is told they are investigating. But this time, in the chard of fire-burned debris of the front bombed-out pews, there is a crumbled note with mismatched sized black lettering spelling out a letter of forgiveness found by the pastor and later given to the police.

CHAPTER 38

WE ARE CONTINUING TO INVESTIGATE

"Authorities are continuing to investigate a bombing and mass shooting at the Pentecostal Church of Harlem this morning that has killed six parishioners and wounded 26 others," the Chief of Police said in front of the 25ᵗʰ Precinct as cameras from the press crowded him. "Authorities do not know what motivated the bombing and shooting."

Suddenly, Tanisha walked over to a reporter from CNN who was standing on the street next to the crowd of cameras.

"May I talk? I was nearby when this happened," she asked. "The violence has devastated this section of Harlem where everybody knows each other."

"My mom saw the gunman run into the church. There was an explosion and then shooting. People were running. They were bleeding," a young girl cried to the reporter into the microphone, "and I can't find my brother! He was there for services."

"I'm heartbroken," the local Pastor Logan with black robe and Bible in hand said with tears. "I've served this community for thirty years. You just never know when things like this are going to happen."

CHAPTER 39

HORRIFIC ACT

By noon, the Chief of Police called an official press conference at the 25th for members of the community, the press, the mayor's office, and officers from several local precincts to the conference room.

"Family and friends of the bombing and shooting victims are waiting in the community center next door with the Red Cross," the Chief of Police said, wiping the sweat from his brow. "The FBI is currently on the scene and the field office for firearms and explosives are on the way. This is a horrific act. And folks, we do not have a lot of information to go on at the moment."

CHAPTER 40

NEWSPAPER DEBRIEFING

"According to the police reports, the church sanctuary was bombed first at 8:30 a.m. The shooting began immediately after," Tom, the editor, said to his roundtable of reporters in his office.

"So, we are looking for someone with precision and timing. Precision and timing for both the bombing and the shooting," Tanisha commented.

As Tanisha spoke, a tall gentleman walked into the room, covered with a dark gray hat and gray overcoat and took a seat at the back of the room.

The room grew silent wondering who the visitor was.

"Is that you, Jonathan? What are you doing here? You are not part of our news team," Tanisha said.

"I thought I could help. I have my press pass. I gave you all my business cards. I was here during the last press conference with the police."

"This is a private news conference," Tom said as he stood up. "How did you get in here?"

"I'm a freelancer here in the city. This is horrific. I'm just trying to help. Your secretary let me in, I have my press credentials."

"I'm sorry, you need to leave. I'll escort you to the front door," Tom said calmly as he walked Jonathan outside past the secretary's desk.

CHAPTER 41

MARCUS

Later that afternoon, when the sun was descending into a deep orange glow, Tanisha took a walk alone from her apartment into Harlem to the hull of the bombed-out church front. She stared at the empty shell at the front of the building as black crows descended dancing in the sky and imagined the people singing gospel there. Their songs were now whispers of spirits in the near darkness.

There was a young Black boy of about seven close by staring with her. It was as if his gaze permeated the yellow police tape crossing the sidewalk with a superhero vision, mesmerized. Then as he finally looked down while kicking the dirt, he found a small object. He picked itt up and twirled the object between his small fingers and then placed it in his palm. It was round and blue and white with swirls and looked like the Earth from a Mother spaceship in the heavens.

"What's that?" Tanisha asked as she kneeled next to the boy.

"Lady, it's called a marble," he said as he put it closer to her face.

"My dad used to think marbles were glass worlds like planets in the night sky."

"My dad used to sing God has the whole world in His hands like this marble here that looks like the world. But he died this morning when the shooter came."

Tanisha gasped and reached out her arms into a hug. "What is your name, son?"

"It's Marcus."

"I am so sorry, Marcus. God does have the whole world in His hands and He will soon come quaking loud and furiously to establish a day of justice," Tanisha said and hugged him again. "Where is your family?"

And Marcus pointed to the community center next door.

"Let's go in there. I'll come with you. I want to meet your family."

CHAPTER 42

DREAMING WHILE BLACK

The dreams and nightmares of Black and Brown women between the police are real. Some lose their lives and property through illegal home searches and unjustified criminalization.

Dreams coincide with the cop culture in which they occur. But in the private realm of self-expression within the collective unconscious, dreams are free. Here, Tanisha has the recurrent dream of freedom and civil rights:

Her neighborhood is stripped of its usual signs of order where she is disoriented, but she remembers the words of Dr. Martin Luther King; "I have a dream."

These are the only words she is able to write and remember as she scribbles them in graffiti on stop signs, school buildings, offices, and malls. Exhausted, she collapses back into the dream and wakes up refreshed. For she realizes that her active role in today's contemporary journalism for truth is not the place for losing sleep.

CHAPTER 43

A MURDER

"A group of crows is called a murder, but there is something more going on inside their instinctive brains. Crows are creepy with a reputation for gathering at funerals. They recognize their dead by gathering in large groups of birds together and mobbing or scolding with loud intense calls of mourning," Tanisha read to Renee.

"So, is that why there is a bunch of crows gathering around what is left of a shell of a church near the 25th precinct? Are they here for the funeral at the community center this afternoon?" Renee smirked.

"You've seen them too?"

"Thought they were pigeons, but no. I know a crow when I see one and there's a bunch of them there just screaming."

"And crows have the ability to memorize dangerous faces. They alarm call and dive bomb when they sense trouble. The crows key in on the face. Crows learn from their peers that the person is dangerous."

"Are you saying those crows know the shooter?" Renee asked.

"I'm saying that the crow won't forget."

CHAPTER 44

FUNERAL

A mass of Latin words falls upon the facts like soft snow, blurring the outline and covering up all the details.

> ~ George Orwell

The benediction at the church was just recorded as another instant replay of White violence, but the Black victims were buried now and gone. They never got a chance to rise again and return to life. Their lifelessness is a grave shadow of permanence.

CHAPTER 45

PREACHING TO THE CHOIR

"Remember ignorance increases as newspapers decline," Tanisha reminded at the morning news meeting, "And we need the truth in news more than ever. It can save lives."

"You're preaching to the choir," Max, an older reporter, said.

"I'm hoping journalists can stay alive," Tom, the editor, remarked. "The politics nowadays is crazy. Everybody has a political opinion. We must now stand as the conscience of news if democracy has any chance at all."

"Yeah, truth trumps!" Stephen, the intern, said.

"I wouldn't say it that way. Trump's biggest enemy is the truth," Renee corrected.

"Word," Tanisha chimed in.

"And I told you all, you are preaching to the choir. Stop preaching at me! Stand tall," Max said. "Constitution over Corruption."

CHAPTER 46

AMERICAN UNIVERSITY

S he was screaming and then shouting, "This is my home, my dorm room! I belong here. What are you doing? Someone help me!"

And students on campus immediately started filming from their phones to help.

Seven White campus cops forcibly removed her Brown body handcuffed behind her back, wrangling violently like a caterpillar from the front door of the building at American University in Washington.

The situation, now under review by the university board, determined her innocence today. Gianna was deemed not guilty of any charges after she was falsely accused by another student of assault.

A local protest by DC students, faculty, and community members took to the streets in a #DayofOutrage.

"This misapplication of force by the police can lead to sanctioned murder," a student observed. "Our lives are at stake."

CHAPTER 47

THE GUNMAN

"So, what are we dealing with today? And what story are we writing?" Tom asked everyone in the newsroom sitting at the conference table.

"There is always the wrong assumption—the perpetrator is always a minority. Not in this case. They saw the White gunman run away," Max, the older reporter explained as he wrote the information onto the white board.

"I'm new at this and don't have a clue," Stephen, the intern said, as he shrugged. "I know medical reporting."

"That may be useful sometime sooner than later," Tanisha said.

"How do we know we are not dealing with a random White cop who is deliberate in their planning through the mind like narcissistic sociopaths living in the moment?" Renee, the youngest reporter, asked, tapping the pencil on the table.

"There is a White gunman whose methodology is precision. The reports show he is capable as a bomb maker and sharpshooter. He knows tactical warfare. He is most likely a person who hates minorities. He is a White supremacist. All of the motives are here," Tom said as he finished writing on the white board.

"But that White supremacist could harbor deep feelings as a cop and use his position to carry out the hate," Renee added.

"Yes, but I think a lot of the White cop violence is carelessness. This is different. It is well planned and deliberate. Like I said, precise. Too precise. Let's look at the letter of forgiveness. What does it say? What are we missing?" Tanisha asked as she wrote again on the white board.

"Wait," Tom said as he stood up next to the board. "We have three crimes in the same neighborhood. Similar looking letters saying the same thing: 'Please forgive me.' Similar looking letters of forgiveness: the prostitute, the woman leaving her door ajar, and now the Pentecostal church. What are we learning? What is the killer or killers telling us?"

"One, it is one killer. And oh my, the act of forgiveness is life-threatening and ends in death. Does that mean more will be killed? Are we being executed by the ideology of supremacy? And who is next?" Tanisha asked deliberately.

"Any one of us. No, precisely us," Max, the older reporter, said. "This person knows us. He knows the neighborhood. We are exposed to him in more ways than we know."

"That scares me," Tanisha said. "We are reacting to his notion of forgiveness. Why? Why does he take his time telling us about forgiveness?"

"Whatever you do, do not give me a hug," Renee said sarcastically.

"Let's think some more. It's been a long day and it's late. We can start again tomorrow morning, first thing. I hope you all are also keeping up with your regular news assignments for the paper. We must not print this investigative story yet, for fear of the gunman," Tom suggested as he wiped his tired eyes.

CHAPTER 48

TRUMP SHOOTS JOURNALISTS IN FAKE CHURCH VIDEO SHOWN TO SUPPORTERS

There is a propaganda video circulating and now trending on Twitter showing Trump disconnected from humanity in the depiction of a mass shooting of journalists inside a church. Americans have been slaughtered in churches, synagogues, schools, and newsrooms for the families to complete the stories of horrors painted upon the American landscape.

~ TV anchor, MSNBC

CHAPTER 49

A CRAZY VIDEO

"Did you see that crazy video on TV last night? We are living in the horror of an American landscaper," Tanisha said, "right here in Harlem. Look at the blown-up church down the street from us."

"Yep, welcome to America," Tom said, cleaning his glasses.

"Come on, you guys. This stuff is serious. It's tough stuff," Stephen, the intern, complained.

"And so, I wonder how cops can walk up to a White mass shooter and put the cuffs on him without incident. And a single unarmed Black person in their own home is threatened. Then killed in cold blood in the dark. Dead like that. American has lost its soul," Tanisha told the other reporters at the Columbia University café.

"I'm saying there is no soul for America. It's a prison abolition system of wealth for Whites," Renee said, sipping her juice slowly. "And you know asking White people if they are White supremacists is like asking the police to investigate themselves for corruption. Now why would we do that?

Suddenly, there was a gasp of silence at the table.

"As you were," Renee concluded.

CHAPTER 50

MAN OF PRECISION

"Let's try this again," Tanisha said during the afternoon meeting as she wrote on the white board, this time in red. "There is a White supremacist who is the silent killer in the darkness of Harlem."

"Spare us the dramatics. Get to the point," Max complained.

"Okay, all of his victims have been Black females and he befriends White cop killers who execute…" she continued.

"Not always, he killed a group of church folk," Renee said.

"Do we know if he is acting alone?" Stephen, the intern, asked.

"No, but the uniting factor is the notes of forgiveness. That's like his personal signature to his crimes of supremacy," Tanisha explained, taking her blue glasses off.

"So, who is the man of precision? The man with the perfect timing. And will he strike again? I have more questions now than answers," Tom, the editor, said.

CHAPTER 51

THE KEY

Tanisha was excited to get to the next morning meeting in the newsroom as she ran up to the white board and started writing. Her fellow reporters leaned in to hear what she had to say.

"This man of precision we have been talking about…. He is the connection between White violence and Black forgiveness. He is the key! White violence is substantiated through his belief in supremacy. He is asking for your Black forgiveness through his notes left at the crime scenes. This allows for his repeated violence. He is looking to perform another act of violence. The letters are a warning asking forgiveness and justification for the White violence he causes," Tanisha explained as the entire news team nodded.

"We need to tell someone," Stephen, the intern, said.

"And who might that be? The cops? Yeah, let's fill out a police report," Renee said as she sucked her teeth.

"We are on to something now," Tom, the editor, said. "Say nothing. Stay alert. Maybe we can stay with a partner for a few nights. Be careful."

CHAPTER 52

MASS BRAWL

Several Transit officers attempt to control a mass brawl of teenagers in the subway. One Transit officer lands a punch in the face of one teen who is just reaching for his backpack. Then he throws him to the ground in order to handcuff him. Suddenly, there are six Transit officers on the floor on his back holding him down. "I can't breathe. Help me, I can't breathe!"

A five-million-dollar lawsuit is now pending against the city. A lawyer for the family has launched an independent investigation.

"The NYPD has no business investigating itself," the attorney said.

CHAPTER 53

YELLOW SIGNS

Large yellow signs waving in protest say "Stop Police Brutality! Poverty Is Not a Crime!"

Hundreds of people come out in the streets to protest this evening against the NYPD violence against Black and Brown people in the subways. People chant, "Shut this racist system down!"

CHAPTER 54

TURNSTILES

The protests against the NYPD policing the MTA continue into the next night by mass hopping of the turnstiles. Crowds of people helping others climb over.

CHAPTER 55

NIGHT WORKER

She is disguised as a night worker in a blonde weave with tight leather leggings, walking. She is seen through the windows as black shadows. She is portrayed as an accomplice working. Some think she is an angel. Lord knows, Harlem needs more angels in the darkness of the night.

And she walks alone in solitude, swinging her red purse from side to side. High heels clicking the pavement in a pace of the clacking harmony of the subway below.

The act of forgiveness is life-threatening and, for her, ends in death as a reality and simultaneously as film does on a screen.

CHAPTER 56

SURVEILLANCE

It's not about the fares. It is about surveillance. Orwell and Big Brother, watching. Now the city installs cameras in front of every turnstile.

CHAPTER 57

MISSED CALLS

"I've been calling you and you haven't returned any of my calls," Jonathan said as he sat down at the Columbia University café. "I'm worried."

"Look, I've been busy. Cops are crawling all over the place since the church bombing and shootings," Tanisha said as she cleaned her glasses. "So, what's so important? Why do you need to talk? How are your stories coming along?"

"I've been busy, but I'm not getting much done getting my freelance work published. It's a hard market here in New York. Thinking about going back to Princeton where I went to undergrad. My friend has some leads on a job with a small paper called *Town Topics*."

Jonathan fidgeted and put both hands in his suit pockets.

"Sounds like a plan." Tanisha sipped her coffee. "And…"

"I'm just having such a time with my editors here. I get too meticulous with my words. A persistent repetition of words," Jonathan said nervously.

"Like how?"

"Like too exacting."

"You mean precise?"

"Yes, exactly," he said excitedly.

"Exactly exacting!" Tanisha laughed.

"Yes, like that. So, how's the work on the church bombing?" Jonathan smiled, "I haven't seen anything big yet."

"Nope. You know the drill. We are investigating." Tanisha sighed.

"Can I help at all?" Jonathan said, now fidgeting with his pencil and tapping on the table.

"Hey, how much caffeine have you had today? You need to lay off the stuff. It's probably not helping you write."

"Yeah, write? Right," he chuckled, concealing his hands behind his back.

"I've got to go. Good to see you. Have a good time visiting Princeton, if you go." Tanisha got up and waved, leaving the café table.

CHAPTER 58

TAKING OVER THE SUBWAY

We are invincible together.

~ Twitter, November 2, 2019

CHAPTER 59

YOUTUBE

The YouTube video was originally filmed by a right-wing troll whose mission was to embarrass the protestors. Then it became the highest viewed video of the day on Twitter because people cared enough to start this in their own cities.

CHAPTER 60

MARATHON

The New York City Marathon plowed through all five boroughs Sunday morning. More than 50,000 runners took to the streets for 26.2 miles, which means New Yorkers may have a few obstacles to get around due to street closures.

CHAPTER 61

REFLECTION

In 1962, Malcolm X said, "The most disrespected person in America is the Black woman. The most unprotected person in America is the Black woman. The most neglected person in America is the Black woman." And it still rings true, almost 53 years later. Today, Black female victims continue to be the most invisible in the darkness of America until the cops see them.

CHAPTER 62

IMPROPER CONDUCT

Records obtained by the *Columbia Herald* show after a two-year-long investigation of improper conduct by two White officers, no criminal charges filed after a Black woman died in police custody. The NYPD released disturbing video last week showing the final hours of a 25-year-old Black female as she died of an overdose. The video shows the woman in obvious distress asking for help as she was shoved into a jail cell.

The *Internal Affairs Unit* found the two veteran officers guilty of improper conduct. One officer has been with the force for fifteen years and the second officer has served for twelve years.

The videos came as a shock to the family and members of the Harlem community.

"Neglect caused her death," her mother cried.

"We want an independent investigation. There is no justice and no peace until we have all the facts," the family lawyer said.

CHAPTER 63

THE COLUMBIA HERALD

"Tanisha, the article you wrote yesterday for our *Columbia Herald* was well done and well researched," Tom, the editor, shared with everyone at the morning meeting. "There will of course be further investigation as this case is also complicated. I think we need follow-up interviews."

"I'll volunteer," Max said as he raised his hand.

"I'd like to assist," Stephen, the intern, added.

"Good idea," Tom agreed.

"It's so difficult to cover police corruption in this city," Tanisha complained.

"I know and we are trying to write better stories and get better coverage and I think all of you are working overtime to make this happen," Tom said.

"It's just a hard beat to cover." Renee shook her head from side to side. "A hard beat."

CHAPTER 64

STOP AND FRISK

Bloomberg's stop and frisk policy for the NYPD resurges again as he considers a presidential bid for office in 2020. The aggressive use of this policing strategy has resulted in millions of Black and Latino people being stopped on the streets unnecessarily. His viewpoint disparages minorities and women with a lack of introspection as the most glaring of his mistakes.

CHAPTER 65

VERTIGO

I stand upon the precipice of the underworld waiting in a land where the faces do not rise like the sun from the newspapers buried in the lede. And the lights swirl a vertigo dizziness around me. Then on the platform flicker melodic silver screeches of steel whirls as we pass solemn through the greatest misery called isolation, in a city crowded with the single repetitive tapping of a foot out of synch, out of time, hollow in despair.

"There is someone stalking me here," Tanisha thinks in her head.

She nervously looks around at the empty subway car as she gets off.

CHAPTER 66

THE BACK ALLEY

It is a cold, brisk morning. And a tall White man walks up and down the back alley close to the 25th precinct. Within the small narrow space of brown red-brick scaffolding upwards, he can peek and see the early traffic along with several crows perched above on the telephone wires.

After putting the garbage into the bent beat-up silver cans, he disappears through a basement door, slipping through the cracks of the city fortress into the darkness. There is a single lit bulb buzzing surrounded by gnats in the hallway.

With his large awkward hands, he grabs the rusted doorknob and closes the inner sanctum. His nervous hands return to the kitchen table equipped with an old black 1960 AM radio playing the morning scratchy hissing news. His hands move more calculating as he assembles the smaller parts. Rubbing his hands together, he makes them warm and flexible to handle the screws. He is a genius mechanic making motors run like machinery as in the preparation of battle bombs having the power to explode as fireworks do in the night.

CHAPTER 67

REAR WINDOW

There is an uncanny silence of the rushing rocking subway car like the feeling someone is watching her on the night ride from the theater home.

And the lady in black leather with red heels is seen as before, disguised in her blonde wig when she enters into the subway car standing in the rear, peering backwards out the window.

But her presence is momentary. Tanisha can only see her from behind as the woman walks toward the opening of the opposite subway door on the side, slithering to disappear into the shadows as she works the night.

CHAPTER 68

STALKING

"Someone is stalking me," Tanisha told Renee at the morning news meeting.

"I believe we are all being stalked on this assignment," Renee retorted.

"You don't understand," Tanisha said as she grabbed Renee's arm. "I have this feeling someone is following me on the subway. That's the only place I feel it. Watching me. It makes me nervous. Look at how I'm trembling."

"Oh, honey. You ARE trembling. What's the matter?" Renee sat Tanisha down on the couch in the newsroom lounge.

"It's everything. I'm afraid something bad is going to happen again," Tanisha said, wiping the blonde curls from her face and taking off her glasses.

"Hey, how about I stay at your house for a few nights and keep us company?"

"Sounds good. Sounds like a plan."

CHAPTER 69

FBI

FBI agents have arrested a suspected White supremacist in Colorado who wanted to bomb a synagogue.

White supremacy remains a major threat to America. This Nazi sympathizer told the agents he wanted to start a holy war.

~ Twitter, November 4, 2019

CHAPTER 70

THE IDENTITARIANS

Another group that promotes its own race and identity in America as a movement is responsible for more than one third of White supremacist propaganda on college campuses in the 2018-19 academic school year, as noted by the Anti-Defamation League.

CHAPTER 71

BLACKFACE, WHITE MASK

The depth of racism is at the heart of American society. And racism is the psychosis. It is the disorder that interrupts thought and emotion, so contact is lost to external reality. White supremacists fit the mask in that they experience this psychosis through the long history of blackface.

Through the mocking of Black people in hideous laughter of drunken revelry on college campuses, they persist in a current crisis of a society moving behind the scenes in a frenzied solitude.

The White supremacist as the center of the universe exhibits a delusional centrality. Staging the power of blackface is to mimic, the permission to mock which authenticates his delusions about himself. He worries about his unwarranted loss of privilege because he is the pathological myth that has the power to destroy his inner soul.

CHAPTER 72

PRINCETON TRADITION

Princeton's tradition of slavery originated with the Pyne family. Moses Taylor Pyne was a benefactor who graduated from Princeton University in 1877 and gained a seat on the Board of Trustees. Pyne's estates were intrinsically entangled with the largest sugar plantations in North America, supported by the work of the enslaved in the South and in Princeton. His wealth allowed him to settle on the estate of Drumthwacket, which is now the official residence of the governor of New Jersey.

Pyne was a member of twelve eating clubs, including the Triangle Club on Prospect that featured minstrel shows with faculty and students engaged in the practice of blackface.

The Pyne House on Winant and on Drumthwacket were opened to the public last week as Tanisha took the tours to explore the depths of the plantation mentality haunting her present.

CHAPTER 73

THE TIGER TEA ROOM

Hidden within the famous maze of the Firestone Library in Princeton University is the black and white checkerboard floor like Alice in Wonderland filled with teas of possibilities and pastry cakes.

Tanisha knew about the special delicacies and found a seat in a red chair by the large corner window. She was worn out from trampling through mansions and Princeton Clubs and just needed a few moments to enjoy her afternoon tea. As she sipped her favorite blend, she thought she heard her name. It was a name similar to hers, but not quite clear.

"Tanisha!" the voice yelled as it came closer. "What are you doing here? I didn't expect you to be here at my alma mater," Jonathan said nervously, putting his hands in both suit pockets.

"What? I'm not good enough? I'm a member of the Ivies, a Columbia grad at that," Tanisha said as she wiped the blonde curls away from her eyes.

"So, what brings you here?" Jonathan said as he straightened his red tie.

"Journalism research," Tanisha said bluntly. "And you?"

"A frat party and a news interview," he said, placing his hands behind his back.

"You party a lot, don't you?" she asked, taking off her blue glasses.

"Doesn't everyone? Maybe you need more of it," Jonathan smirked.

"Where's your frat? The Triangle on Prospect?"

"How would YOU know that?" Jonathan asked suspiciously.

"Just figured. You're a big frat guy. Heard a lot about Princeton's wild life," Tanisha said sarcastically. "You must have laid off the caffeine. You're not as nervous today."

"Yes, less coffee, more beer," Jonathan chuckled. "You should try it."

"Hey, I must get back to the city," Tanisha said as she wiped her mouth with her napkin. "Have fun at your frat party," Tanisha said as she left Jonathan behind in the Tea Room.

CHAPTER 74

CROW'S FEET

It was a sudden look of amazement. Tanisha noticed a synchronicity in the crow's feet etched in the frozen cement of the sidewalk. It was as if the crow had signed his own signature.

"Look, Renee, I noticed this a few days ago and wanted to show it to you," Tanisha said as she bent down and pointed at the sidewalk.

"Okay, an imprint of crow's feet," Renee said.

"When do you think these were made here in the cement, I mean?" Tanisha asked.

"I guess we could find out when the city laid the cement. Looks like it was a recent job 'cause the cement is a lot whiter than the other slabs," Renee said as she took a photo.

"These few slabs are on 126th near the alley of the 25th precinct. I'll check it out," Renee said as she took another photo.

CHAPTER 75

SIDEWALKS

By the next day, Renee had already checked out the replacement of sidewalk near the precinct. "Hey Tanisha," she called on her cell phone, "I have some answers for you. The sidewalk is fairly new, about five years old. It was replaced by the city due to large tree roots breaking the first sidewalks. They replaced several slabs, about fourteen in total I guess. In the process, a crow stepped into the cement making these crow prints. I'll send over some photos so you can see. This crow has its own signature style. Do you think this crow is trying to tell us something? Do you think we are dealing with some crooked cops here?"

CHAPTER 76

FOLLOW THE CROWS

"Follow the crows. First, let's make sure to count all the slabs of sidewalk. There are fourteen crossing the front of the 25th precinct, pass the alley and then in front of the Pentecostal Church storefront. Notice all the crows sitting on the telephone wires here, watching. And let's check who has been on the police force for the last five years." Tanisha said to Renee as they took photos again and walked along the sidewalk.

CHAPTER 77

DOUBLE VISION

"Everything has been pretty stagnant," Tom, the editor, said as he updated the staff at the morning meeting and scratched his head.

"I thought we might notice something during the vigils and funeral," Max said as he sipped coffee, "but no leads."

"I do think I am being stalked," Tanisha told the newsroom. "There's this same woman that seems to appear on the #1 subway every time I am down there. She has a blonde wig with dark skin and tight clothing, high heels."

"How do you know you are stalked?" Tom asked.

"Hmmm. Blonde hair and dark skin like you?" Stephen, the intern, said.

"Now, that's being creepy!" Tanisha shouted across the newsroom.

"I think we are all being watched," Renee said. "This is a high-profile case, you know."

"Have you noticed strange people around? People you don't know?" Tom asked as he leaned in to everyone.

"Crows. There are a lot of crows around the bombed-out church, the 25th precinct…" Tanisha said.

"Not crows. People," Tom said deliberately and shook his head from side to side. "Where would a White supremacist hide in Harlem?"

"A college campus," Tanisha perked up. "I was just at Princeton and there's a lot of blackface stuff going on there. And here at Columbia too. I filled out a police report there."

"And there's been a lot of racist propaganda about White supremacy on campuses lately," Stephen said.

"When you have something more credible, call me. And be careful," Tom said as he left and closed the newsroom door.

CHAPTER 78

GENDER PAY

Collectively, women and Black reporters should not earn less for who they are. Gender pay disparities are the most pronounced among journalists under the age of 40.

- Washington Post Guild, 2019

CHAPTER 79

PROSTITUTION

Several prostitutes stand inside the 96th Street subway trying to stay warm from the heat of the outbound subway cars. They giggle as they push each other into an empty car that arrives at the station. The lady with the blonde wig and dark skin is the last to shove her way past the other ladies and sits alone chewing a wad of gum, smacking her bright red lips. She opens her red purse to reapply her make-up and looks off into the distance with a blank stare through the rear window.

CHAPTER 80

VANISHING POINT

The doorbell rang.

"Are you expecting an Amazon delivery?" Renee asked.

"No," Tanisha said as she finished making the lentil soup.

Then they suddenly looked at each other and did not move as if they were frozen in time. And then they listened. Tanisha wiped her hands with the dish cloth and walked towards the door.

"That's weird," Tanisha said looking at the intercom video. "I don't see anyone out there." Then Renee joined her in looking at the video.

"There is nothing there, but the doorbell did ring," Renee said.

"Well, the front door has two deadbolt locks," Tanisha said as she locked the door. "That's what locks are for. Come into the kitchen. Soup is ready!"

CHAPTER 81

AN AMAZING MOMENT

Lester Holt receives the honor of the *Walter Cronkite Award for Excellence in Journalism*. "This is an amazing moment for American journalists and it demands clarity and fearlessness."

~ Twitter, November 4, 2019

Tanisha and Renee watch the television intensely this evening because of the meaning for all journalists writing at this turbulent time in American history.

CHAPTER 82

SHADOWS OF A DOUBT

"Okay, there are five White cops who recently started working for the 25th precinct in Harlem during the last five years," Renee told the news team at morning meeting. "They are Richard Hunt, Timothy Deal, Peter Zelenski, James Browning, and Carl Muncy. They are all in good standing," Renee stated.

"All except for Carl Muncy who we should be keeping an eye on," Tanisha explained. "He is the one just fired from the force not too long ago for shooting a Black woman through the back bedroom window in her own home. He is charged with murder and out on bail. And looking through his file, he was a high-risk hire who, when asked will you be able to kill if you had to said, he had no problem doing so. He also owned four firearms and joined the force after a career in engineering. We all were there during the press conference earlier this year," Tanisha said as she looked everyone in the eye.

"Those are red flags," Tom nodded and put on the white board. "He should have never been hired."

CHAPTER 83

FRENZY

It's garbage day and he comes out of the back alley like clockwork as a tall white mechanical soldier on the pedestal of a cuckoo clock, pacing in circles. This is the way he takes out the large black plastic bags of garbage filled with debris in a nervous pacing, waiting for the deep hum and clang of the New York City garbage truck.

This morning, a single black crow recognizes his face from the telephone wire and swoops downward between the buildings to attack the man in a frenzy. The beak pecks and penetrates perfect near the eyes now bleeding into his face, dripping due to the dive bombing and scolding attack. He runs screaming holding his face as he runs into the darkness of the basement.

The abrupt healing of the wound tends to scar as he calms down to finish the mechanical assembly of the precious timer.

CHAPTER 84

BLACK CONVERSE AND RED HIGH HEELS

They entered the darkness onto the subway platform at the same time from opposite ends of the tracks: black Converse sneakers and red high heels.

The red high heels quick pacing with a clicking echo as Converse moves in silence. But they suddenly stop and peer at each other, noticing a similar mirror image reflection of the same curly blonde hair, dark skin, and blue glasses. And the woman who wears the red heels boasts a hideous laugh that regurgitates the subway tunnel blackness as the #1 train grinds to a halt into the station.

And they both disappear in a simultaneous step forward like a country dance do-si-do into the emptiness of their own train car, both staring away out of the rear window.

CHAPTER 85

PHOTO

"That lady was stalking me again last night!" Tanisha shouted. "She stared right at me as if she knew me!"

"You should take her photo next time. Make sure she isn't a delusion," Max said jokingly.

"You are not funny!" Tanisha shouted back at him. "I was too scared to take her photo. It was a good thing I had sneakers on. I could run away."

"But you didn't," Max retorted.

"It would be tough for her to run after you with high heels. I suppose she wears stilettos?" Renee said. "The shoe of choice for women of the night. She's probably not thinking about you at all."

CHAPTER 86

HEARTBROKEN

Just a month ago, he had sat down with reporters heartbroken over the shooting death of his daughter by a cop in Harlem at her own residence. "I don't want no hug," he said. "That was my one and only daughter. I will never forget that."

And her father passed away today. He died of cardiac arrest. But he really died of a broken heart while today's police violence rips apart the hearts of an entire community.

CHAPTER 87

ANOTHER POINT OF VIEW

Several Transit cops encircle a Latina woman selling Churros in the subway. She begins to cry when they demean her in English as she tries speaking to them in Spanish.

Some who live by the same subway witness the incident and take video and post footage on Twitter. Quickly, Julia Salazar, state senator for New York, sends her team to Transit District 33 reaching out to the Chief of NYPD's Transit Bureau to intervene in the woman's behalf.

The woman is released with just a civil summons. And Salazar thanks everyone who saw the incident and responded in a positive manner for standing up.

CHAPTER 88

COPS SWARM TEENS PAST MIDNIGHT

The *Columbia Herald* reported today that ten days ago, teens were detained after midnight for three hours by cops without parental notification and then arrested after an evening of trick or treating.

A witness reported one boy hit by an unmarked black car driving the wrong way down the street. Another witness said cops pulled out their guns to scare the teens. The seven teens involved are all Black.

"The cop's actions are reckless. This is the kind of policing that keeps parents up at night. God knows what can happen," a parent who wished to remain unidentified said.

CHAPTER 89

THE PROFILE

"This should be a productive meeting today. Again, Tanisha, your investigative reporting on the teens detained on Halloween was excellent. Keep up the good work. Now, let's get back to the other story: determining motive. Who has enough hate to kill several people in Harlem's Pentecostal Church? Some of you have good leads," Tom, the editor, began the meeting.

"So, there was White male who got away. So, there is one solo mass killer and bomb maker. He is the profile we are dealing with," Max, the older reporter, read from his notes. "There's a possibility that a NYU professor that has been in the news lately fits the profile. He promotes hate on his radio station as he doubles under an alias. He welcomes the far right with open arms."

"But does that make him a prime suspect? I wonder how many White supremacists are lurking around in this city," Tanisha said.

"He is guilty of hate speech. Not enough to convict," Stephen, the intern, added.

"Any other evidence?" Tom asked. "Keep working on this and give me a call when you figure it out."

CHAPTER 90

WE NEED EVIDENCE

Later that afternoon, Renee and Tanisha met together in the newsroom.

"Okay, now that we figured out the timeline for the cement slabs of sidewalk within the five years of cop history, let's take a closer look at what's there in the photographs," Tanisha said as she spread the photos across the table of the newsroom. "What do you see?"

"Hmmm. The front of the 25th precinct, an alley way, a staggered group of crows on the telephone wires, then the bombed-out shell of the Pentecostal Church. All in front of this newer sidewalk. And so?" Renee asked, scratching her head.

"What do they have in common?" Tanisha said, taking off her blue glasses.

"It all smells of White supremacy to me as the motive for the bombing and shooting. But the cops said the guy got away."

"But that does not mean he isn't around. I think he is familiar with the neighborhood. Maybe he is hiding in the subway, underground, or in the precinct with some White cops or in an alley. The crows know that there is a villain in our midst," Tanisha said cautiously.

"Then follow the crows," Renee said. "Seriously."

"So, start in the alley next to the precinct tomorrow afternoon where the crows live. We need evidence. Assumptions won't help us or others in Harlem against the hate. Bring Max and Stephen with us, but let Tom know where we are going. Someone needs to know," Tanisha said.

CHAPTER 91

UPRIGHT HANDS

A clock whose hands are upright at twelve breathes the infinity of a second in time. Here, one lies between the thoughts of a philosopher like Dr. King with the momentary pleasure of peace.

CHAPTER 92

OUR DEEPEST FEELINGS

One lends things our deepest feelings. Tanisha throws her shawl onto the back of the kitchen chair after a hard day of work overthinking. As her warm red shawls grabs the chair back sloping, it embodies a form feeling empathy with the bodies of people passing by and interviewing voice to find the story of the city. Exhausted, the shawl drapes limp losing its warmth into the bare metal back of an old kitchen chair now as it has grown frozen cold.

CHAPTER 93

ALGORITHMS OF OPPRESSION

The most powerful lines of computer code are called, google. And its masterful algorithms control the results one sees into powerful distortions of misinformation. Every minute, 3.8 million requests are made using this internet tool. Google engineers make the behind the scenes adjustments to alter the results. Users beware.

CHAPTER 94

FILM NOIR

I t is like a film scene. Dark dreary subtle lights play against the background of water dripping as single steps walk a quickening pace. Then slipping through the slither of a doorway at the south end of the subway into Penn Station at 34th, an architectural masterpiece. These are the last remains of tile work constructed in subway tunnels of 1908 by Guastavino. Tanisha scampers the stairwell as a 1950s still of a film noir with its crisp elements of shadow and stark harsh light as a flashback of an American crime drama. And with the echo of each footstep forward, there is someone who secretly follows.

CHAPTER 95

CANDY FUNDRAISERS

It was 7:30 pm on a Friday evening when four officers brutally attacked a teen for selling candy from his school in the subway. One should be appalled by the violence and criminalization inflicted by the NYPD on a daily basis. This reflects a systemic disorder of policing in the city.

CHAPTER 96

FINGERPRINTS

The NYPD maintains a secretive database of fingerprints that labels thousands of unsuspecting minority youth as gang members based upon arbitrary and broad criteria. The police have violated the law in fingerprints for years without consequence. Legal Aid attorneys discovered juvenile record keeping of these prints and the need according to the law to destroy these records. NYPD officials continue to stonewall the Legal Aid attorneys from doing their jobs.

CHAPTER 97

A SINISTER SYLLABUS

There is an overwhelming movement toward racial exclusion and white power ideology. He speaks a fluency in white nationalism and anti-Semitism as he writes speeches and makes policy. Now there is proof from the *Southern Poverty Law Center* in the form of 900 leaked emails, the key advisor for the president, Stephen Miller, is drowning in an unapologetic white nationalism. In this camp, white supremacy rules.

CHAPTER 98

HATE CRIMES

The number of hate crimes reported by the FBI during 2018 increased to heightened levels. A newly released study exposed 7,120 hates crimes as reported by law enforcement. The data released shows the greatest bias against African Americans.

CHAPTER 99

MANIFESTOS

Racist manifestos are airdropped onto the phones of college students in the library at Syracuse University causing alarm. Nowadays, White supremacy attacks our society in waves of high profile shootings or bombings followed by copycat impressions. But this new wave marks the first of the internet savvy digital minds of young men who can spread hate to the masses with tremendous speed with unsuspecting propaganda accelerating toward a mad irrational hallucinatory future.

CHAPTER 100

AMERICA'S FRATERNITY CALLED RACISM

P ledging and rushing breed a chasm of segregation that permeates
a collegiate society. The White fraternity system appears in a
bubble of resources which creates the spaces of Eurocentric ideology
and practices. With little or no cultural competence, there is a lack
of integration for diversity as a powerful White alumni class emerges
to produces the healthy donations for their institutions.

CHAPTER 101

POLICING POST-ITS

Multicolored post it notes display their stick-to-itiveness underground against the white tiles of subway walls on 14th Street in an artist installation called, Subway Therapy. The artist, Matthew Chavez, is a regular feature of enjoyment for two years here. But today, he received a ticket from the MTA and NYPD officers because he is not in compliance. Straphangers who travel underground disagree and encourage his artistic free speech with a thumbs up.

CHAPTER 102

A TELEVISION MOMENT

Mister Rodgers broke the color barrier when he dipped his feet in the same pool of cool water on a hot day with Officer Clemmons on the set of *Mr. Rodger's Neighborhood.* In 1969, Black and White people could not swim in the same pools. Today, the country revisits the event in a new movie celebrating love in this neighborhood on TV.

CHAPTER 103

MIRANDA RIGHTS

Contrary to what ones sees in the movies, police do not need to read the Miranda warnings before you are arrested. But they do have to read them to you during interrogations. And one should never speak to the cops without a lawyer.

CHAPTER 104

THE CULT OF TRUMP

Today's picture is much darker. The Cult of Trump is more extreme and depraved. For it is just the beginning of a wild ride on a political rollercoaster. Be prepared to hold on.

CHAPTER 105

IMPEACHMENT INQUIRY

US Representative, Adam Shiff said, "There is nothing more dangerous than an unethical president who believes he is above the law. And I would just say to the people watching here at home and around the world, in the words of my great colleague: We are better than that, Adjourned!"

CHAPTER 106

TOWN CRIER

Newspaper reporters used to be the backbone of local journalism. As print revenues plummet, so does the interest in the newspaper which covers its communities, leaving people with misinformation or no information at all.

The first draft of history must continue to be written in order to keep democracy accountable. The town crier must cry loud again. It means our existence or extinction. Journalists must seize the day, the moment of vibrancy breathing, to keep the news truthful and alive.

CHAPTER 107

LEAVES LIKE HANDS

That day was an extremely windy one. And he had been watching the leaves in the alley way from his window. They were blowing furiously in the opposite direction, crashing into his face first, then his feet as he rushed out the basement door. A military man on a mission, he seemed headed toward a catastrophe. He blew pass Tanisha on the sidewalk almost shoving her. But she passed him by unknowingly in the opposite direction. And he didn't look back.

CHAPTER 108

SLY EYES

The alley sneers at their presence breathing an odor of guilt as the four approach. And the little windows of the basement below the three doors is elongated like a sly eyes watching. They have entered this dark space as the intruders of white fairytales. Wicked is its being now an existence as it comes into a dragon's life.

CHAPTER 109

ALLEY OF SECLUSION

During the late afternoon, the light from the sun is blocked by the building on one side of the alley in deep dark shade next to the precinct. Clotheslines and telephone wires hang criss-crossed directly above the tight space, creating high-tension wire scaffolding that holds the wings of birds in attention watching every movement below.

As they enter the alley, they disappear from view as they quietly squeeze pass crushed garbage cans filled with black bags full. Then, they step over Coke cans and crumpled-out freshly smoked cigarette butts to move toward three doors and one low basement window. The end door is ajar, slightly opened enough, showing the stairs of a dark descent beneath a single light bulb swinging.

As they move through the door, they hear the slight whispering of jazz music of Ella Fitzgerald on an old stereo album hissing and scratching, then crackling as they reach for each other holding hands. The four follow the stairwell slithering to the bottom to finds a small kitchen with table, chair, and radio with intricate bomb-making parts somewhat assembled.

Stephen gasps with his hand over his mouth as Tanisha takes

photos of the bomb-making scene. Max joins in taking photos of the entire basement. But it is Renee who is mindful that the suspect may be away for a very short time and gets Tanisha's attention with a soft whisper.

CHAPTER 110

NO WAY OUT

"There is no way out of the building except through the front lobby. But we take the risk of being seen. We are already trespassing. We need to call the cops to get us out of here."

"No, the cops will shoot us! Either way, we'll be dead," Stephen screamed nervously.

"Shhh. You need to be quiet," Tanisha said as she was quickly contemplating thoughts and then at the exact moment of synchronicity, she had a new plan of action. "Stand still and text the precinct next door for help. Let them know we will come out with our hands up," Tanisha explained.

Slowly they raised their hands above their heads after they sent the 911 text. Then she carefully walked toward the lower basement window and opened it. As the cold air penetrated the room, the light illuminated their faces in the darkness. And they stood still, frozen, waiting.

After three minutes, red and white flashing lights flickered through the alley onto the side of the opened basement door. Six cops entered the basement yelling, "Put your hands above your head!"

And upon seeing their petrified faces from the flashlights and minimal sun, they led them outside one by one into the alley.

"You found bomb-making materials?" one of the cops asked.

Tanisha and the others nodded and two cops went back inside. As the cops searched the home, they took digital evidence of photos with racial violence and video of someone firing at a mosque, along with an arsenal of guns, ammunition and documents for making bombs.

And then the blood-curdling screams as a woman with blonde hair and blue glasses in blackface in a black leather dress and heels was dragged from the basement into the light of day. The fierce movements of her body squirming and fighting off the cops caused her wig to dismantle, leaving a partial man's haircut in view hanging. A close-up look at the face revealed the pecking marks of crows. And in a high-pitched woman's voice, she screamed, "This is my home! You can't take it away. I will sue the city! I live here!"

And Tanisha screamed and cried simultaneously at the mirror image of herself.

"That's the lady who follows me. She stalks me! NO? Who are you? Jonathan? But you are a man. No, a woman? I am so confused! You are wearing blackface! I don't know who you are! Are you crazy? What's wrong with you? You tried to kill us. Oh, my God! This is a nightmare!"

CHAPTER 111

IDEOLOGIES

The landscape of the mind is psychological. Monsters lurk in the deep dangerous vaults of the far-right political resurgence. These ideologies that support Trump's notion of fake news are at work against the truth. Merchants of hatred in this American context seek their inspiration from such aspects of scorn.

CHAPTER 112

A DEVASTATING SHADOW CAST

When the moral compass of a nation moves backwards, the decline of its values is already in motion. White supremacy is terrorism if allowed to fester and attempts to undermine the unity of democracy. One must understand this significance in the attainment of power in order to ask the following pertinent question, "What is next?"

CHAPTER 113

CHURRO CARTS

The cops arrest an older Latina woman at a Churro cart selling snacks. And it is not illegal to sell food inside a subway station. The police obviously pretend not to see the hundreds of newsstands and Churro carts that define the New York City subway.

CHAPTER 114

RALLY

We are coming together to say NO to over-policing, YES for fair working conditions for vendors, and YES to subway and bus improvements.

Be there:

Monday, Noon

~ Broadway Junction subway, November 11, 2019

CHAPTER 115

SOCIOPATH

It was the music, the jazz that Jonathan played as monsters lived in his head that made the delusions of hate come out alive like a horror movie. And for just a minute, Jonathan was one and the same in White supremacy as the assassin and sociopath in blackface who attended Princeton University.

In the end, his blonde wig disheveled remains hanging, now exposing the short male haircut he wore underneath as he is handcuffed without incident and taken to jail like the other mass shooters and bombers projected on TV.

CHAPTER 116

TRAPPED

The image of blackface had become Jonathan's reality at Princeton and Columbia through the minstrel shows and drunken bouts hidden in the darkness of his fraternity parties at the Triangle Club on Prospect. And in this dark side of his personality, he festered a hatred for African Americans. For in his mind, he was superior as a supreme spiritual being as White. Always looking for the opportunity and finding the motive to finally allow the hate to kill innocent Black people walking alone or on the streets or in the Pentecostal Church on 126th Street. It is here in this hateful state of mind his White supremacy becomes terrorism.

In the solitude of his personal exile, he morphed into the delusional persona as a glamorous Black female, a being so opposite living in the depths of the night as a prostitute. And as time went on, becoming more delusional as he is now, psychologically trapped forever within the mirror image of his female counterpart, Tanisha.

CHAPTER 117

ENDLESS DAYS OF WHITENESS

As Jonathan sat on his bed in a catatonic stare, he could still see the trees and huge hickory leaves like hands wringing the necks of black crows scrambling outside his window. The leaves floated and flew whirling in the wind. It was raining leaves on this windy day as he lay on his back dazed in whiteness of a coma of nothingness called sleep. And the rest is silence.

CHAPTER 118

OBSESSION

In his heart, he was strangely bound in love for Tanisha, to admire her from afar for being the journalist he always wanted to be. Tanisha was the woman he could never have; he could never be. He embodied her in blackface with the blonde wig and blue glasses. He imitated her in dress and in mannerisms, but just could not control the nervousness of his hands.

So, Jonathan kneels and prays with rosary beads slipping through his fingers nervously every evening, asking for Black forgiveness.

CHAPTER 119

POSSIBILITIES

"I'm really going to quit this business," Tanisha told her editor, Tom, as she closed the newsroom door behind her and walked away facing west with her dark gleaming face raised brightly toward the sun. And in that moment, everything bathed in radiance.

CHAPTER 120

After the arrest and conviction, she is left in deeper psychosis at the mental facility in upstate New York. Her face contorts, laughing at the image in the looking glass. For somewhere back there in her mind is shouting the hideous ramblings about her majestic perfect life in Princeton. Jonathan speaks louder in the voice of a woman as if lost in a bad dream.

EPILOGUE

For there is a thin line between the geniuses, the psychotics and the sage. The sage knows he/she is changing their reality but the psychotic does not know and remains trapped in the deceptive world of the hallucination but the genius always knows the difference.

The fragmented mind can never know reality because it always exists divided.

APPENDIX A

THE DIVINE AND THE DIABOLICAL MASCULINE

The story represents the mythical and diabolical masculine aspects of a criminal story. His black female victims are invisible in the darkness until the police officer sees them. But film itself erases their existence by not bothering to show them as human as they truly are. When White supremacy goes unchecked, it becomes this delusional space that illuminates and occupies part of a society like film. For whiteness is the hidden accomplice that fosters the violence one sees onscreen.

There is further emphasis placed upon the plague of I and the Other which causes the injustices within society. This brings us to reckon with question, Is there a secret to healing the feminine as she gains power through self-sufficiency; the archetypes which emerge from this personal story?

As one shifts in mind of our stories, as archetype of the feminine instead of the masculine, a new reality emerges in the collective unconscious (Campbell, Joseph). There is the search for social justice through inner peace of the reflective mind in the midst of chaos.

References:

Myths to Live By. New York: Viking Press, 1972.

The Mythic Image (Bollingen C). Princeton, NJ: Princeton University Press, 1974.

APPENDIX B

THE EMERGENCE OF THE FEMININE

As women, one cannot escape our destiny in gender. The dismissal of a women's gender suffering is a reason for a legal redress. For so long, women have been rendered as trivial after enduring harassment, violence and rape at the hands of men in society. A shift is important for the current political and legal implications to change. Women who are silenced are now are finding the words to speak out.

Today, the great themes of mother, healing, and power are coming into view. But we are still left suspended in the heavens, leaving our stories open and unfinished. This gateway opens to the never ending stories all around us. Carl Jung called this juncture, the inexhaustible energy of the universe in our world of dreams as we sleep in the darkness of the collective unconscious (Jung, Carl). Upon awakening, the feminine gives birth in the love of the ultimate unity consciousness of story. This power of intention orchestrates its fulfillment in the nonlocal field of synchronicity. And when we engage in the source of our empowerment.

We as the empowered feminine, discover there is no end to

the eternity of our lives as we birth the singing of the song of our unfinished stories. For we must tell our stories.

References

Jung, Carl. An acausal connecting principle. In *Collected Works, 8: The Structure and the Dynamics of the Psyche* (2nd ed.). London, UK: Routledge and Kegan Paul, 1969.

Jung, C. *Carl Jung, Letters Vol. II* (pp. 108-109).

APPENDIX C

SYNCHRONICITY: QUANTUM CONSCIOUSNESS IN THE EXTREME

" In time-travel research, we are exploring extreme situations in which space and time are warped in unfamiliar ways" (Gott, 31). Space-time, the concepts of time, and three-dimensional space are regarded as fused in a four-dimensional continuum. Mass tells space-time how to curve and space-time tells mass how to move.

In the same way, quantum physics disturbs our normal way of thinking about time in our reality but proves to be true on the subatomic scale in physics. It is like *Alice in Wonderland,* objects may disappear and tunnel into another space in time or appear distorted and unexpected to the reality of the human eye.

Carl Jung and Albert Einstein laid the foundation for this notion in 1905-1912 with their discussion of synchronicity and physics. In the quantum field, consciousness can travel the speed of light from the future into the past and back into the present using Einstein's theory of relativity now supported by quantum mechanics.

My study of the field of astrophysics and the theory of relativity at Princeton University during the years of 2016-2018 helped me to connect the concepts of synchronicity together. This book relies on this theory as part of the foundation for the book's premise in synchronicity and consciousness, the moment of coincidence that signifies the mastering of time travel.

Quantum Leaps in Princeton's Place, Six Doors Down, The Future Is My Past, Time Is the Length to Forever.

REFERENCES

Bartusiak, Marcia. *Einstein's Unfinished Symphony: The Story of a Gamble, Two Black Holes, and a New Age of Astronomy*. New Haven, CT: Yale University Press, 2017.

Chopra, Deepak. *Quantum Physics of Time*. Carlsbad, CA: Chopra Foundation, 2013.

Gott, J. Richard. *Time Travel in Einstein's Universe: The Physical Possibilities of Travel Through Time*. New York, NY: Houghton Mifflin, 2001.

Halpern, Paul. *The Quantum Labyrinth: How Richard Feynman and John Wheeler Revolutionized Time and Reality*. NEW YORK, HATCHETTE BOOKS, 2017.

Hartle, James. *Gravity*. San Francisco, CA: Benjamin Cummings, 2002.

Penrose, Sir Roger, and Subhash Kak. Quantum Physics of Consciousness. *Journal of Cosmology*, Vol. 3, No. 14 (2012).

Schutz, Bernard. *A First Course in General Relativity*. LONDON, ENGLAND: Cambridge University Press, 2009.

APPENDIX D

CREATIVE WRITING AS A GESTURE IN SYNCHRONICITY

S cholarly Presentation and Published Paper at American University in Paris, France, June 14-16, 2017

Synchronicity is serendipitous creativity. Moments in time when events come together to create product, it is art as gesture, in this case, creative writing of my novel, *Six Doors Down*. The creative trilogy of novels is framed by one of the four levels of inquiry into consciousness, Level 3: Depth-psychological Hermeneutics (Brian Lancaster, 2004).

Specifically, this is representative of Jung's postulate of the collective unconscious. Mental and physical events are interrelated. Physical events can be intrinsically meaningful as in his concept of synchronicity. Depth psychology constructs and religion apply so that the concealed realm reveals itself through a series of meaningful events. Jung argued that this unseen unconscious contains archetypes that function to transmit knowledge to the conscious realm. Space and time are relative; knowledge finds itself in a space-time continuum that is no longer space or time (Jung,

1952b, para. 912). Writing is an artistic gesture that may capture the notion of synchronicity in the product as literature.

Synchronicity is about coincidence in single moments of time. In synchronicity, a moment unfolds the normal sequence of clock time. We experience extraordinary moments of timelessness through the experience of the conscious mind. Through my research and study at Princeton University, I discovered that synchronicity is the window, the key—this moment in time. Time travel into the future or past and back again to the present takes place in the quantum field and consciousness of mind.

Synchronicity is quantum. In physics, the quantum field is the unifier of all consciousness. Jung connected support from physics for his psychological theories. Jung confirmed that his work was influenced and connected by Einstein's theories of relativity in physics (Jung, 1935, para. 140). His theories mimic aspects of Einstein's theory of relativity. Einstein's theory and the space-time continuum in physics are the sources from which Carl Jung derived the word *synchronicity* (1952b, para. 840).

Another way to think about synchronicity is the ability to distort time, arriving at a destination of thought by skipping steps. As a rupture in time: synchronicity transgresses the way time normally operates. Meaningful connection between events with no perceived a-causal connection. Time through this aspect of consciousness is therefore abolished. Thereby, making the present both the past and the future. The conscious is timeless.

And the novels, *Quantum Leaps in Princeton's Place, Six Doors Down,* and *The Future Is My Past,* are written in a way that utilize the theories of Carl G. Jung and Albert Einstein. Together, these theories suggest the possibilities of time travel into the future back into the present and the past back into the present through the quantum field of consciousness.

The documentation of this experience in synchronicity in creative writing is an artistic gesture of literature and creative work in the humanities. In other cases, the experiences are scientific documentations and writings such as the structure of the atom by Niels Bohr and the benzene ring molecule by August Kekule coming through the unconscious mind. Certainly, Jung believed in this power of consciousness in the human mind in the product of writing.

BIBLIOGRAPHY

Gott, J. Richard. *Time Travel in Einstein's Universe: The Physical Possibilities of Travel Through Time.* New York, NY: Houghton Mifflin, 2001.

Herzog, Michael H., Thomas Kammer, and Frank Scharnowski. Time Slices: What Is the Duration of a Percept? *PLoS Biology,* Vol. 14, No. 4: e1002433. doi:10.1371/ journal.pbio.1002433

James, William, and Kitaro Nishida. *Pure Experience, Consciousness, and Moral Psychology.* Indiana: Purdue University, 2007.

Jung, Carl. An acausal connecting principle. In *Collected Works, 8: The Structure and the Dynamics of the Psyche* (2nd ed.). London, UK: Routledge and Kegan Paul, 1969.

Jung, C. *Carl Jung, Letters Vol. II* (pp. 108-109).

Lancaster, Brian L. *Approaches to Consciousness: The Marriage of Science and Mysticism.* London, UK: Palgrave Macmillan, 2004.

McGuire, William, and R. F. C. Hull (Eds.). *C. J. Jung Speaking: Interviews and Encounters.* London, UK: Thames and Hudson, 1978.

Main, Roderick. *The Rupture of Time: Synchronicity and Jung's Critique of Modern Western Culture.* London, UK: Routledge, 2004.

Ryden, Barbara. *Foundations of Astrophysics.* San Francisco, CA: Pearson, 2010.

APPENDIX E

The great themes are left suspended in the heavens, leaving mythical stories unfinished. It is a gateway to the never ending stories that are all around us. Jung called this juncture, the inexhaustible energy of the universe in the world of dreams as we sleep. With an awakening of the dawn, the feminine gives birth again. And when we return to the source of our empowerment, we find there is no end to the eternity of life for the unfinished story.

References

Jung, Carl. An acausal connecting principle. In *Collected Works, 8: The Structure and the Dynamics of the Psyche* (2nd ed.). London, UK: Routledge and Kegan Paul, 1969.

Jung, C. *Carl Jung, Letters Vol. II* (pp. 108-109).

ABOUT THE AUTHOR

Dr. Donna Clovis is the current Outstanding Book Award Winner in 2019 for NABJ for her first book, Quantum Leaps in Princeton's Place. She has an earned doctorate from Teacher's College, Columbia University in Arts and Humanities. Dr. Clovis has also won two journalism fellowships: McCloy Fellowship from the American Council on Germany and Harvard University and a Prudential Fellowship from Columbia University Graduate School of Journalism. The McCloy Fellowship resulted in producing documentary work about Holocaust survivors in Germany, now archived in the Holocaust Museum in Washington, D.C.

Clovis has won a first-place feature-writing award on racial profiling from the National Association of Black Journalists in 1999.

Dr. Clovis writes historical fiction and fantasy novels about Princeton. Quantum Leaps in Princeton's Place is the first from 1912-1950, Six Doors Down, The Future is My Past, Time is the Length to Forever and the most current, Falling Bedrooms and Just a Book in the Library, dealing with the rise of racism, the death of the American newsroom and challenges of truth and fact finding in a world of fake news.

She is Assistant Professor of English Education for Rider University.